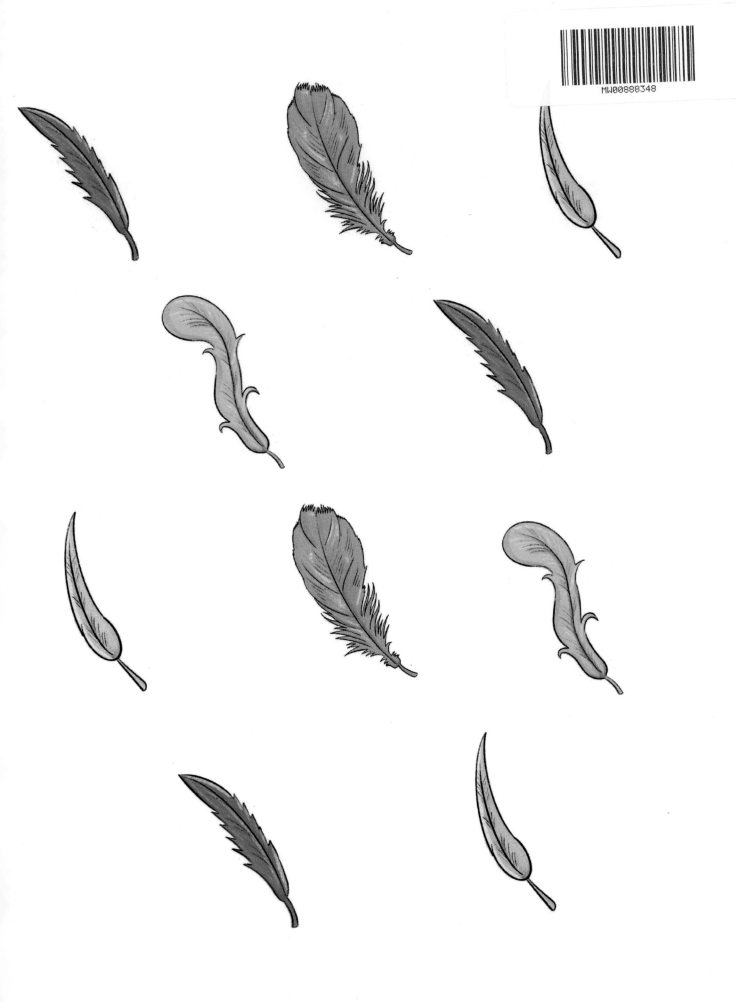

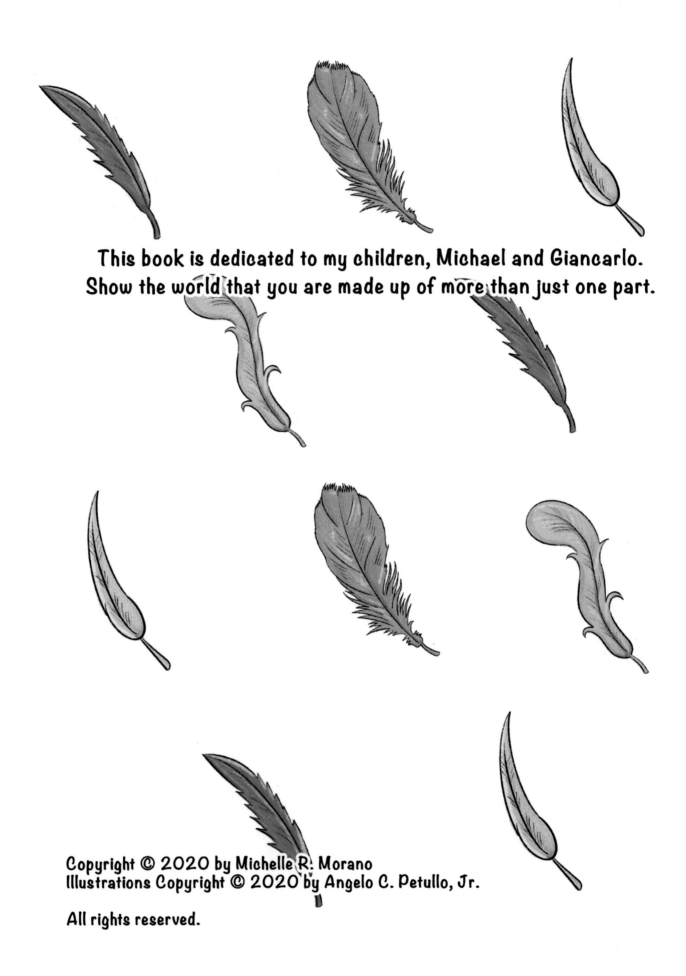

This book is dedicated to my children, Michael and Giancarlo.
Show the world that you are made up of more than just one part.

It's Just Me

Written by Michelle R. Morano

Illustrated by Angelo C. Petullo, Jr.

Rosie didn't waste any time exiting the classroom.
She was the first one out the door, heading home as quickly
as she could, since she did not have a good day at school.
Being at home made her feel better.

On her way home, Rosie passes through her favorite park.
She always enjoys seeing the large, open areas of grass shining in
the sun, the thick towering trees gently swaying in the breeze,
and the many bushy-tailed squirrels scurrying
along the pathways.

Her favorite part is petting the dogs that run up to her begging for
a pat on the head. Walking through the park makes her feel happy
and relaxed, a much better feeling than
she feels when she is at school.

"Why do they point at me and whisper?"
asked Rosie to herself. "It's just me," she answered quietly.

Rosie always thinks about this when the kids at school look
at her and point. She hears them say, "That's the one.
Remember what she did?" It always makes her feel
alienated, lonely and sad.

"It's just me," she said to herself.

She thought back to the time when she made
a horrible mistake; a mistake that everyone seemed
to always remember. It was ONE time in her life when
such a horrible thing happened.

"Why do they only remember THAT about me?"
she asked herself.

Rosie tried to forget about that horrible mistake in her life
as she continued to walk through the park.
As she kept walking, a feather appeared in her path.
Picking it up, she noticed how the multiple shades of yellow and
orange stood out brightly against the white.
"How pretty!" Rosie exclaimed.
"This feather must belong to a beautiful bird."

After walking several more steps, a second feather
appeared. Rosie picked it up and noticed how
the soft pink color of ballerina slippers stood at pointe.
"Ballet," she said. "This feather must belong to a bird
that enjoys ballet dancing ."

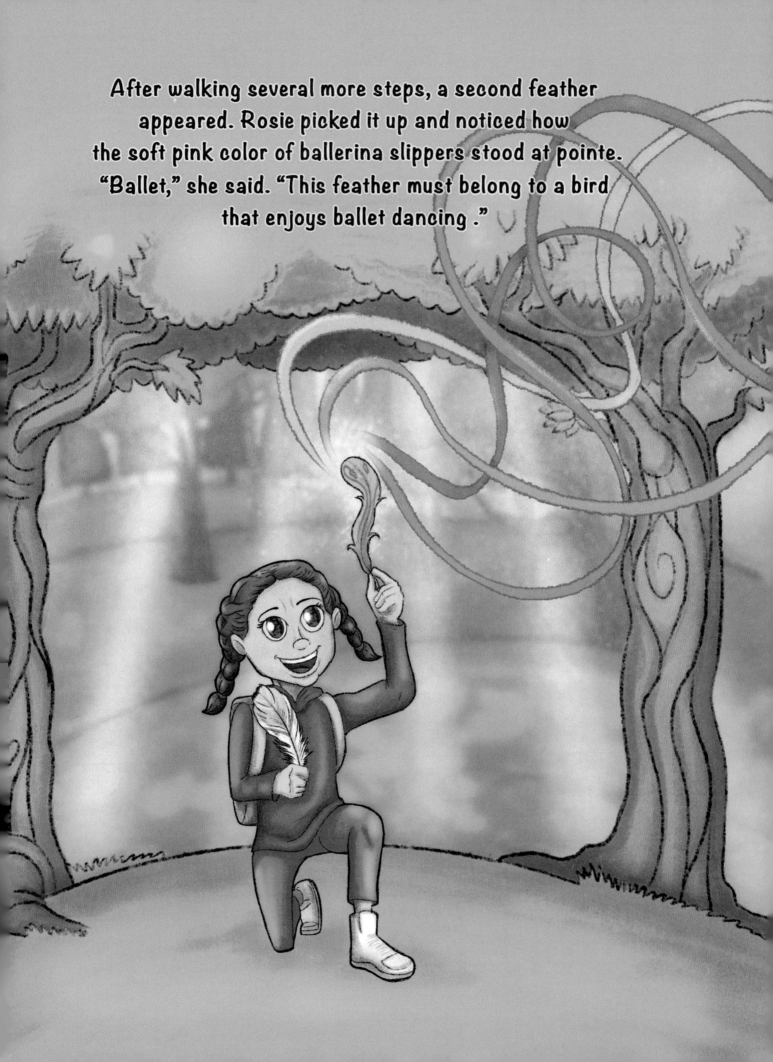

Tucking the feather gently behind the first one,
she continued on her way.

As she rested on a park bench, a third feather appeared.
Rosie picked it up and noticed how different titles of books
stood out against the brown. "Books," she said.
"This feather must belong to a bird that enjoys reading!"

Tucking the feather gently behind the second one,
she continued on her way.

After stopping to pet a dog, a fourth feather appeared.
Rosie picked it up and noticed how the red cylindrical shaped
drum with wooden sticks stood out against the brown.
"Drums!" exclaimed Rosie. "This feather must
belong to a bird that enjoys playing drums."

Tucking the feather gently behind the third one,
she continued on her way.

Rosie became excited as she looked at her hand holding the four feathers. She couldn't wait to get home and show her mom what she had found. "Wait till I show Mom what I found in the park!" she exclaimed with excitement. Her pace sped up at the thought of getting home.

"Mom, Mom!" Rosie shouted as she ran through the front door.
Her mom came running from the kitchen to greet her.

"What, what?" answered her mom.

"Look what I found in the park as I was walking home from
school!" She held out her hand for her mom
to see the four feathers.

"You found feathers?" asked her mom.

"Yes but not just any feathers.
Look what's on each one!" Rosie stated with excitement.

Her mom took the feathers from Rosie's hand
and looked carefully at each one.
"These are beautiful," she admired.
"It looks as if each one has a special print on them."

"They do," replied Rosie. "I found them as I was walking
through the park. Do you think they belong to the
same bird?" asked Rosie.

"I believe they do Rosie," answered her mom.
"I believe this particular bird is made up of many parts and
that's what makes it unique and special," Mom explained.
"Just look at the feathers! This bird is a beautiful bird that likes
to ballet dance, read books and play drums."

"Kinda like me," Rosie added.
"I am made up of many parts," Rosie continued.
"I like to bake, play video games and play soccer."

"That's right Rosie," stated Mom. "That's what makes you
unique and special. It's all the parts put together that
make up a person. It's not just one part."

"If only the kids at school would think that about me," Rosie stated with sadness.

"Maybe bringing those feathers to school tomorrow and explaining what you found will help them see that there is more to you than just that horrible mistake," stated Mom.

"I will and I will even make my own feathers that have the things I like on them!" Rosie stated enthusiastically.

"That's a great idea Rosie," stated Mom.

The next day Rosie brought all of the feathers into school.
She showed her teacher the ones she found
in the park and then shared her own.

"Would it be okay with you if we shared them
with the class?" asked Ms. Ruberto.

"Sure," Rosie stated hesitantly. She was nervous about
how the class was going to react since they always
whispered things about her horrible mistake.

Ms. Ruberto let Rosie explain what was on her feathers.
As Rosie explained in detail about her love of baking, playing
video games and her experiences playing soccer, her
classmates began whispering. Instead of them whispering about
her horrible mistake, they were whispering about how fun it
would be to get together with her to play video games and
bake for the school fundraiser.

Rosie's face beamed with delight.
It was then that Ms. Ruberto said,
"There's more to a person than just one part."

About the Author

Michelle R. Morano fell in love with books at a very young age. Today, she is pursuing her dream of becoming a first time author. When Michelle is not reading she is enjoying ballroom dancing and entertaining her family and friends. Michelle lives in New Jersey with her husband and two children.

About the Illustrator

Angelo has been drawing since the age of four and hasn't slowed down since. He has illustrated multiple children's books and looks forward to continuing his career in illustrating children's books and comics.

Made in the USA
Middletown, DE
17 January 2021